D0819810

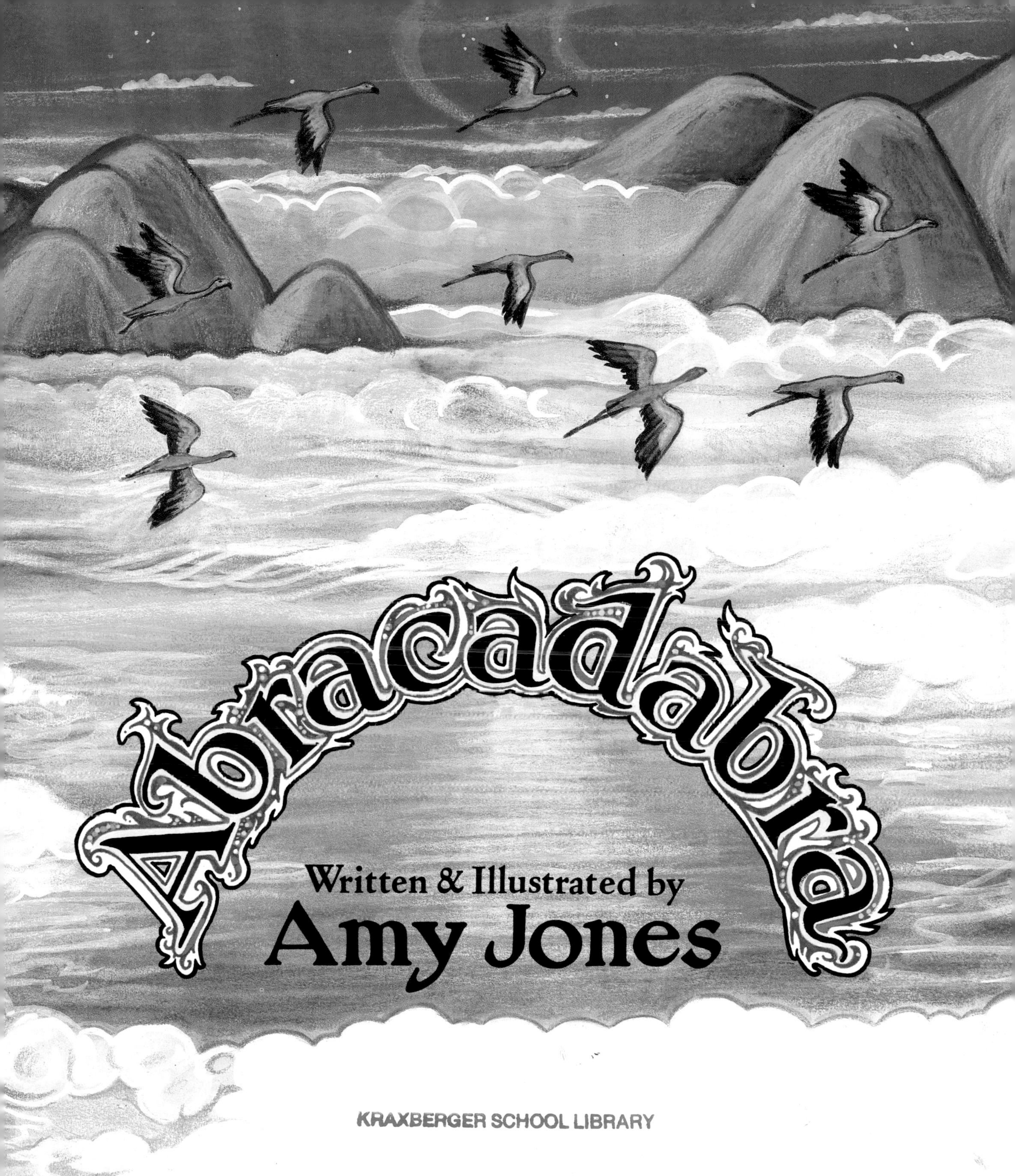

Abracadabra

Written & Illustrated by

Amy Jones

LANDMARK EDITIONS, INC.
P.O. Box 4469 • 1402 Kansas Avenue • Kansas City, Missouri 64127

Dedicated to:
Jane Hawkins, Sandy Smith,
Karen Wildman, James McGinness,
Bill Harris, Kathaleene Bailey,
and Sing Blue Silver.

International Standard Book Number: 0-933849-46-X (LIB.BDG.)

Library of Congress Cataloging-in-Publication Data
Jones, Amy, 1974-
Abracadabra / written and illustrated by Amy Jones.
p. cm.
Summary: After her eccentric Aunt Melissa gives her an enchanted unicorn for her tenth birthday, Katherine uses the beautiful creature's help to try to rescue her aunt from the evil Sultan of Zabar.
ISBN 0-933849-46-X (lib.bdg. : acid-free paper)
1. Youth's writings, American.
[1. Unicorns—Fiction. 2. Fantasy—Fiction.
3. Youth's writings.]
I. Title.
PZ7.J6813Ab 1993
[Fic]—dc20 93-13421
CIP
AC

Editorial Coordinator: Nancy R. Thatch
Creative Coordinator: David Melton

Printed in the United States of America

Landmark Editions, Inc.
P.O. Box 4469
1402 Kansas Avenue
Kansas City, Missouri 64127
(816) 241-4919

ABRACADABRA

Amy Jones is a very skillful writer and illustrator. She is also a very determined young lady. She wanted to become a published author and illustrator so much that she entered our NATIONAL WRITTEN & ILLUSTRATED BY... CONTEST two years in a row. And in the 1992 CONTEST, she entered not one, but two extraordinary books. Her determination paid off when one of her books was chosen by Landmark's editors as a Gold Award Winner in the upper age category. I am delighted that she won and I am pleased that Landmark has published her wonderful book.

Working with Amy was an absolute joy! She was quick to learn, eager to please, and open to suggestions. She always seemed to appreciate our interest in her work and the assistance we offered.

I admire Amy's eagerness to improve her skills as a writer and an artist. I never heard her complain, not even once, about pressing deadlines or the amount of work she had to do to refine her text and illustrations.

As you will see, Amy has created an enchanting story and painted lovely illustrations for her book. If you like to read about beautiful unicorns, delightful cats, eccentric aunts, despicable villains, magic gems, and around-the-world adventures, then you are going to love ABRACADABRA!

— David Melton
Creative Coordinator
Landmark Editions, Inc.

My Aunt Melissa is the strangest aunt anyone could have. She wears brightly colored dresses, big flowery hats, and get this — GLOVES! She *always* wears long white gloves, even when she's eating breakfast. Strange, really strange!

My parents and I rarely see Aunt Melissa because she is usually traveling around the world. She knows all kinds of famous people, such as the Queen of England, the President of France, and the Grand High Lama of Tibet. The last time she was in New York, she had dinner with Michael Jackson.

Anyway, from wherever she is in the world, Aunt Melissa always sends a special gift to me for my birthday. And each year the gift is bigger and grander than the one before.

When I was eight, she sent a large doll house that looked like the Taj Mahal. The next year a troupe of Russian acrobats arrived and performed for the whole neighborhood. Everyone thought they were absolutely wonderful, except my father. He had to pay for replacing the flowers the acrobats had trampled.

Two days before my tenth birthday, I received a note that read:

> Dear Katherine —
> Your present is in the mail.
> I know you will love it.
> Happy Birthday!
> — Aunt Melissa

I could hardly wait for the gift to arrive. Whatever it was, I knew it would be big, REALLY BIG!

The morning of my birthday, I jumped out of bed and ran to our front yard. I looked up the street and down the street. No trucks were in sight. So I went back inside the house and waited.

Just before noon the doorbell rang, and my excitement grew. I rushed to the front door and opened it wide. I had expected to see a giraffe standing there, or an elephant, or even perhaps the skeleton of a dinosaur. But none of these were on our front porch. There was only a delivery man, holding a tiny box in his hand.

"Happy Birthday, Katherine!" he said as he handed the box to me.

I was so disappointed, I could barely mumble a weak thank you to him. I just stood there staring at the tiny box.

"Who was at the door?" my mother asked as she entered room.

"A delivery man," I replied. "I think he brought my present from Aunt Melissa."

"How big is it?" Mother asked with concern.

"It's not big at all," I answered, holding out the box for her to see. "In fact, it's very small."

"Oh, thank goodness, it *is* little," Mother sighed with relief. "Your father will be so pleased. It's not big enough to trample the neighbor's flowers. Well, Katherine," she urged, "aren't you going to open your present?"

I nodded my head yes and took a deep breath. Then I unwrapped the paper, lifted the box top, and looked inside. Nestled in soft cotton was the most beautiful glowing thing I had ever seen — a tiny handpainted porcelain figurine of a unicorn.

"Oh, look, Mother!" I exclaimed. "Isn't it lovely!"

"It certainly is!" she agreed.

"I love it!" I said. "It will look so pretty on the shelf by my bed."

I carried the figurine upstairs to my room, where my cat Cinnibar was napping on the floor.

"Look, Cinnibar," I said. "What do you think of my birthday present?"

Cinnibar yawned and opened his eyes. I could tell he liked the unicorn, for he stretched and smiled the way he always does when he likes something. My father says cats don't smile, but I know Cinnibar does. And after I placed the unicorn on the shelf, Cinnibar walked over and stared up at it admiringly.

When I awoke the next morning, the first thing I did was look at my unicorn. After school I rushed home, because I was so eager to see it again. But when I ran to my room, the unicorn was not on the shelf. Could it have fallen off and landed on the floor? I wondered.

The thought of that made me shutter. I was afraid when I looked down that I would find my beautiful unicorn lying there, broken into a hundred pieces. I was so relieved when I didn't see it on the floor. Then I searched for it throughout my room, but still couldn't find it. I was almost ready to give up when I finally saw it. My unicorn was standing on the windowsill!

"How on earth did you get there?" I wondered aloud.

Just then Cinnibar sauntered into the room.

"Cinnibar-r-r-r-r-r!" I said accusingly. "Did you move my unicorn?"

Cinnibar looked up and gave me his I'm-not-going-to-tell-you-anything kind of look.

"Well, if you did, don't do it again!" I scolded.

I placed the unicorn back on the shelf where I thought it would be safe. But the unicorn never stayed there. Sometimes I found it under my bed; other times it would be on my chair; and one time it was in my house shoe.

"You are like quicksilver," I told my elusive unicorn. "You slip away and are gone before I know it. I think you must be magic. Maybe I should give you a name that has a magical sound to it. Now, let me think for a minute. Oh . . . I know a perfect name for you," I finally said. "I'm going to call you *Abracadabra*."

Late one night I was awakened by the sound of galloping hooves. My room was filled with the glow of moonlight. And I could see that Abracadabra was gone again!

I hurried to the window. When I looked outside, I gasped in astonishment. The unicorn was circling in the yard below. And to my complete amazement, he was no longer the tiny size of a figurine! HE WAS FULL GROWN!

When Abracadabra looked up and saw me, he impatiently tossed his head from side to side and dug his hooves into the grass. I could tell he wanted me to join him in the yard. So I ran down the stairs and out the back door.

As I approached the beautiful animal, I reached out my hand and patted his silky coat. Then I took hold of his mane and climbed up on his back. No sooner was I settled in place than he started to move. He trotted slowly at first, then burst into a gallop and sped across the yard.

When we came to a rail fence, I held my breath. I need not have worried. Abracadabra jumped up and sailed over, clearing the fence top by several feet. Then we raced the moon across an open field and headed for some woods. As we neared the trees, Abracadabra leaped high into the air, taking me over the branches and above the clouds. I was so frightened, I closed my eyes and held on as tight as I could.

"Nice unicorn," I pleaded. "Nice, pretty unicorn. *Please,* let's go back down to the ground."

My wish seemed to be his command, for he immediately turned around and headed for home. When we landed in the back yard, I quickly dismounted.

"Look," I said, trying to stop my knees from shaking, "that was a really neat ride. And I liked the galloping-across-the-field part of it. But, you see, I'm basically a ground person who doesn't like high places. I don't even like climbing up ladders or riding on elevators. So I could have done without the over-the-trees-and-above-the-clouds part. Quite frankly, *it scared me a lot!* So please, don't do it again. Do you understand what I'm saying to you?"

Abracadabra nodded his head and pranced about, but I wasn't sure he got my point. In any case, I turned and wobbled into the house. I clung to the banister as I slowly climbed the stairs. *And I didn't look down — not even once!*

I was awakened the next morning by the sound of my father's voice.

"There's a white moose standing in our back yard!" I heard him bellow.

"I know," Mom replied. "It must have been left there by mistake."

"Well, I hope the neighbors don't expect me to pay for any damages it does!" he grumbled.

"I'm sure they won't," Mom told him. "Now eat your breakfast, George, so you won't be late for work."

As soon as Dad left, I hurried outside to pet my unicorn. But I couldn't find him anywhere. That made me uneasy, and I rushed back into the house.

"Mom," I said, "Abracadabra is gone!"

"That might be for the best," she replied. "Your Aunt Melissa means well, but nearly every time she sends a gift, things get complicated."

"She and Dad never got along, did they?" I asked.

"Well, they're brother and sister, but as different as night and day," Mom explained. "Your father is such a serious, responsible man. Your Aunt Melissa, on the other hand, rarely acts as if she has a care in the whole world."

"Dad says Aunt Melissa is a real scatterbrain," I said.

"He also thinks your unicorn is 'a white moose,' my mother laughed. "Anyway, he doesn't want the animal in the back yard. So you had better find Abracadabra and get him out of sight before your father comes home."

I searched and searched, but Abracadabra was nowhere to be found. Three days passed and he still had not returned. By the third night, I was so worried, I couldn't sleep. About midnight I climbed out of bed and went downstairs to get a glass of milk. I got only as far as the living room because the television suddenly blinked on. Then, in large purple letters, a message flashed across the screen:

HELP!
I'M BEING HELD CAPTIVE!
COME TO MY RESCUE BEFORE IT'S TOO LATE!
—AUNT MELISSA

"But how can I find you?" I asked.

The television blinked again:

THE UNICORN IS IN YOUR BACK YARD.
HE WILL KNOW THE WAY.

HELP

"There are certainly a lot of strange things going on here," I mumbled to myself. But I didn't have time to think about them now. Aunt Melissa was in danger and needed my help. So I put on my coat and ran outside to join Abracadabra.

"I want to know just one thing," I said to him. "Is this going to be a nice-and-easy-run-on-the-ground kind of ride?"

Abracadabra whinnied a reply, but I didn't know if that meant yes or no. But somehow I suspected that we were about to take an over-the-trees-and above-the-clouds trip. I reached up, grabbed hold of Abracadabra's mane, and jumped aboard his back. To my surprise, Cinnibar leaped up and sat down behind me.

"I don't think you should come along," I told him, but Cinnibar refused to jump off. "Then hold on tight!" I warned him as the unicorn began to run.

By the time Abracadabra reached a full gallop, Cinnibar was very nervous. He dug his claws into my coat and began to hiss and growl. I knew he wished he had taken my advice and stayed at home.

After a few more strides, I no longer could hear the unicorn's hooves touch the ground. I knew what that meant — we were airborne! Not wanting to look down, I closed my eyes. But after a while, I became so curious I had to look. Slowly, ever so slowly, I opened them.

Oh! It was the most beautiful sight I had ever seen! The lights from the cities below us looked like flickering jewels that had been scattered across the ground. And the lights of cars flowed like sparkling ribbons along the highways.

"Cinnibar, look at the pretty lights!" I exclaimed. Cinnibar was not at all amused by what he saw. He just hissed and growled some more and held on even tighter.

In time we came to the end of land and began to fly over the Atlantic Ocean. The full moon cast a gentle, mystical light that added to the wonder of our floating on air. The unicorn moved with such grace and freedom that I was soon lulled into sleep. I'm not sure how long I slept, but when I awoke, the sun was rising in the east, and I could see land again.

I couldn't help but wonder where we were. To our left I saw mountains and green valleys. To our right was a large city. Then I saw something I recognized — the Eiffel Tower. I knew we were over France!

From there, we flew to Italy and Greece, then farther south across the Mediterranean Sea. Once we were over Egypt, I could see the pyramids as they sat majestically on the desert sands below.

Suddenly Abracadabra started to descend. Down! Down! Down! we went toward the city that spread out before us. As we sailed over buildings with domes and towers, it appeared as if we were flying into the land of the *Arabian Nights*. And I think we were!

Straight ahead of us stood a magnificent palace. The unicorn flew directly toward one of the tallest towers of the building. The closer we got, the more frantic I became!

"Look out!" I finally screamed. "We're going to hit the tower!"

My cry of alarm made Cinnibar hiss and growl even louder. But Abracadabra kept his course and aimed for a barred window that was near the top of the tower.

Then, just as we were about to crash into the bars, the strangest thing happened — we shrank! That's right, we shrank! It was like *zap!* In a moment's time we were small enough to fly between the bars, which we did! Then, no sooner had the unicorn landed inside the room, than *zap!* We were normal size again!

The experience of changing sizes completely unnerved me. I slid off of Abracadabra's back, glad to be alive. Cinnibar growled in annoyance, then jumped into the safety of my arms.

"Thank goodness you're here!" I heard a familiar voice say. I turned, and there stood Aunt Melissa, handcuffed and chained to a wall.

"Aunt Melissa!" I exclaimed. "What's going on here?"

"Hello, Katherine, Darling," she replied. "So glad you could come. You *must* help me get out of these horrible chains before the Sultan of Zabar and his awful guards return. You didn't happen to bring a hacksaw, did you?" she asked.

"I'm afraid not," I sighed.

At that point Abracadabra jumped into the air, and *zap!* He shrank to a small enough size to enter the keyholes in the handcuffs. Within seconds the first cuff was unlocked, and Aunt Melissa's left hand was released.

"What a clever unicorn!" Aunt Melissa exclaimed.

"I call him *Abracadabra,*" I told her.

"A most appropriate name!" she said and smiled her approval.

Then, before zapping himself back to regular size, the unicorn quickly unlocked Aunt Melissa's other handcuff.

"Oh, that feels much better," she sighed. Then, with great aplomb she straightened her long white gloves, picked up her hat, and placed it neatly on her head.

"Meow!" mewed Cinnibar, announcing his presence.

When Aunt Melissa saw Cinnibar, she exclaimed, "Ohhhh, what a beautiful cat! And what a wonderful idea to bring this marvelous creature with you. He's just what we need!"

"Need for what?" I asked. "Cinnibar is only a cat."

"He may be just a cat when he's at home, but while he's here, Cinnibar will be our secret weapon," she said and laughed her rollicking laugh.

I still didn't understand, and I don't think Cinnibar did either. But he loved the attention and purred with delight.

"Why don't we just get on Abracadabra's back and fly out of here before the Sultan discovers us?" I suggested.

"We cannot leave without the blue sapphire," Aunt Melissa said determinedly.

"What blue sapphire?" I asked.

"The one the Sultan stole from me," she replied. "You see, it's a most unusual jewel because it has the power to control a person's mind. With this stone, the Sultan could force thousands of people into slavery. And he would do just that because he is truly an evil man."

"Where did *you* get the blue sapphire?" I asked.

"From Lord Rankin, a wonderful old English gentleman. When he became ill, he wanted to make certain the jewel would be placed in safe hands. So he asked me to take it to the Grand High Lama who lives in the Himalayas.

"I hid the sapphire in the headband of my hat," she continued, "and left Lord Rankin's home. But on the way to the London airport, two of the Sultan's men forced my car off the road and pulled me outside. They taped my mouth shut, tied my hands and feet, and rudely dumped me into a large trunk. Then I was loaded onto the Sultan's private airplane and flown here. When I arrived, the Sultan took the sapphire and imprisoned me in this miserable tower!"

"But, if he has the sapphire, why won't he let you go?"

"Because," she explained, "he needs the three words that can activate the power of the stone. He won't release me until I tell him those words."

Suddenly Abracadabra whinnied and pawed the floor.

"I think we are about to have visitors," said Aunt Melissa, and she quickly placed Cinnibar behind a screen. "You stay there until we need you!" she instructed.

"Meow!" Cinnibar said in agreement.

When the door was opened, four guards entered the room and stood at attention. Then, from the darkened hallway, a man wearing a fancy turban and silken clothing stepped forward.

"Aha!" said the Sultan of Zabar. "I see you have company."

"Katherine is my niece," Aunt Melissa informed him.

"It must be nice to have a family reunion while you're in prison," he smirked.

"It would be even nicer if you would return the sapphire to me and let us be on our way," my aunt replied.

"Then tell me the three words," he demanded, "and you will be free to go."

To my surprise, Aunt Melissa told him, "You don't know it, but you already have the three words. They are inscribed inside the sapphire. All you have to do is hold it up to the light, and you will see them."

"Aha!" the Sultan said gleefully. And he took the blue sapphire from his pocket, held it up to the light, and looked into the jewel.

"I don't see any words," he complained.

"Keep turning it," Aunt Melissa said sweetly. "It must be held in just the right position for you to see the words."

The Sultan of Zabar turned the stone again and again.

"I still can't see the words!" he fussed impatiently. "Here," he said, handing the sapphire to Aunt Melissa. "You find them for me."

Aunt Melissa held up the sapphire and began to turn it. "I can almost see the words, but not quite," she said, squinting her eyes. Then she suddenly stopped.

"What's that?" she asked as she looked around the room.

"What's what?" the Sultan wanted to know.

"That smell!" she said, sniffing the air.

"What smell?" he asked.

"Do you have cats in the palace?" Aunt Melissa inquired.

"Absolutely not!" the Sultan replied emphatically. "There are no cats in the entire city. They are forbidden! I am allergic to cats."

"So I've heard," Aunt Melissa said with a sly smile. "But all the same, I think I smell a cat right now, and I think it's in this very room."

"Nonsense!" exclaimed the Sultan. "If there were a cat nearby, I would be . . . AH . . . I would be . . . AH . . . AH . . . I would be . . . AH . . . AH . . . AH CHOO! . . . *sneezing* There *is* a cat in this room!" he shouted and sneezed again. "Guards, find that cat! AH CHOO!"

Before the guards could do anything, Cinnibar jumped over the screen and landed on all fours on top of the Sultan's turban.

"AH CHOO!" the Sultan sneezed again. "Get this cat off of me!"

The guards drew their scimitars. But before they could attack, the unicorn, being the magnificent animal that he is, rushed into action. He bravely placed himself between the guards and Cinnibar, and with his sharp horn, he engaged the Sultan's men in a sword fight.

As the blades of steel slashed at his horn, the unicorn dodged to the left and charged to the right. I was so proud of Abracadabra! One by one, he quickly knocked the scimitars from the guards' hands and forced all four men against the wall.

Then Cinnibar, being the independent cat that he is, reached down, and with one of his exposed claws, he pierced the very tip of the Sultan's nose.

"Yeowww!" yelled the Sultan.

"Cinnibar!" I warned. "That's enough! You come here right now!"

Cinnibar ignored me and began to shake himself so that loose cat hairs fell all over the Sultan. Then he jumped down and came to stand beside me, looking very pleased with what he had done.

"AH CHOO!" the Sultan sneezed. "*Please,* get that cat out of here!" he begged.

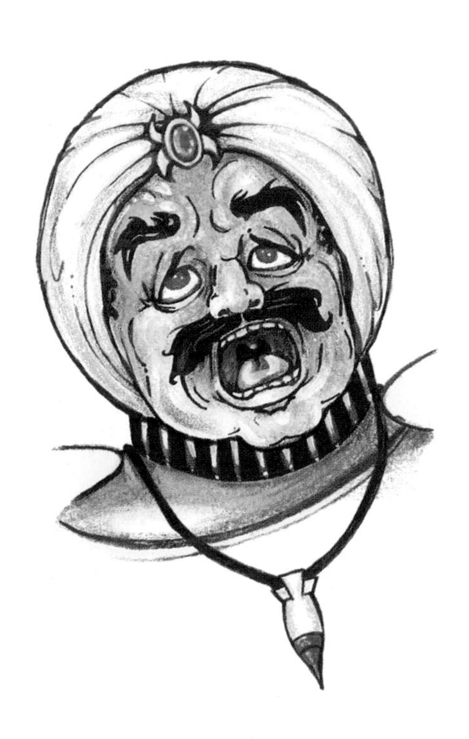

"We'll be happy to," Aunt Melissa told him, "but only under certain conditions."

"And just what are your terms?" the Sultan asked arrogantly.

"You are a very wicked and greedy man," Aunt Melissa scolded. "You have built up a great treasury, but your people go hungry and live in wretched shacks.

"All that stops today!" she ordered. "From this day forward, you will use your wealth for the good of your people. You will feed the hungry and build houses for the poor."

"And if I refuse to yield to your demands, what can a silly old woman like you do about it?" he sneered.

Aunt Melissa straightened her back and said sternly: "You must do exactly as I have said, or we will stand here and watch you sneeze yourself to death!"

"AH CHOO!" the Sultan sneezed again and again, until he was so weak, he fell to the floor. "Okay!" he moaned and wheezed, "I agree to everything. Just get that cat out of here!"

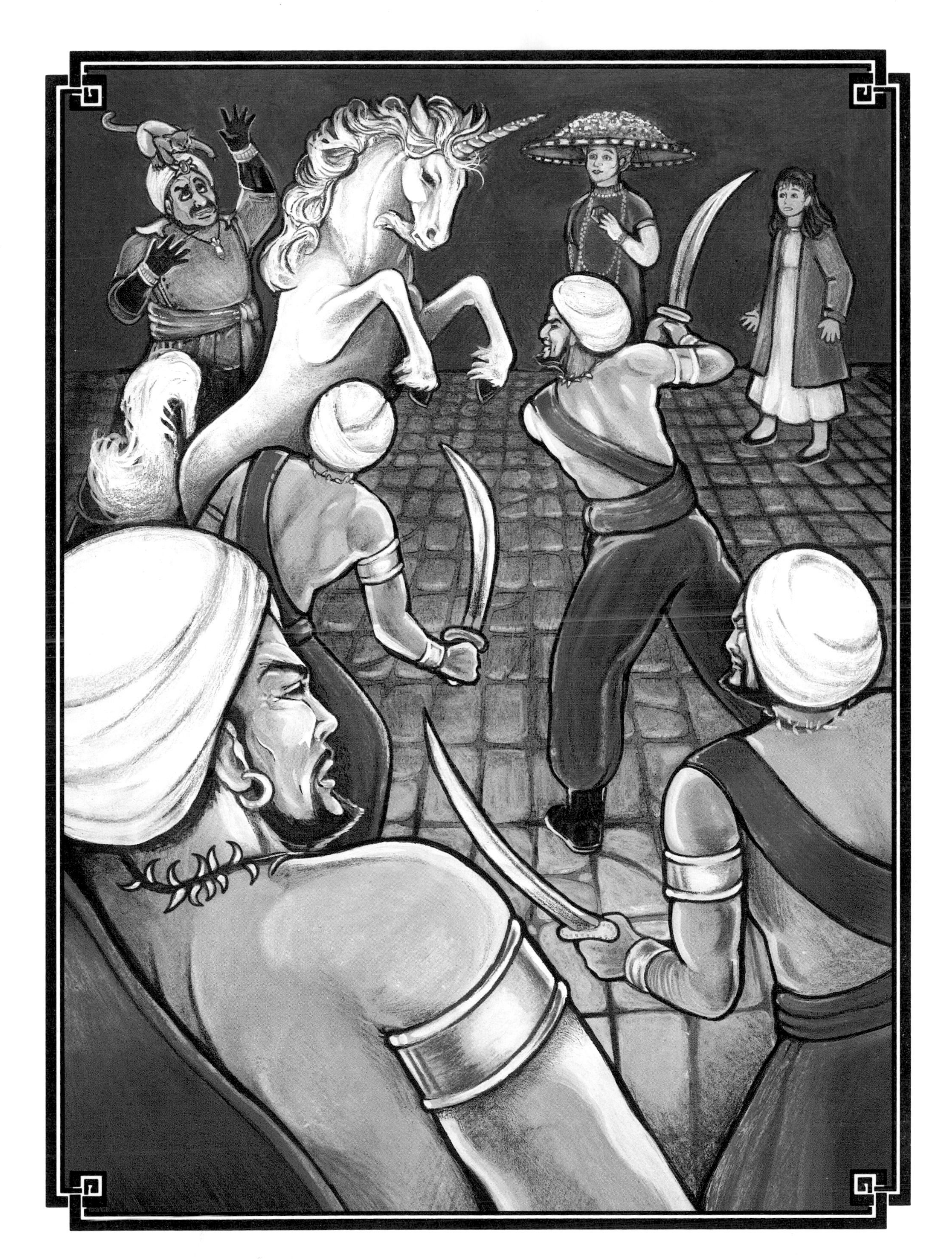

"We will be happy to do that," Aunt Melissa told him. "But if we ever hear that you have not kept your word, our unicorn will bring more cats to your palace — hundreds of cats with nice long fur, just for you!"

"No! No! I promise!" the Sultan groaned. And then he sneezed again, "AH CHOO!"

Aunt Melissa tucked the blue sapphire into her headband, and we climbed onto Abracadabra's back. "To the Himalayas!" she commanded. And *zap!* We were small enough to fly between the bars. Then *zap!* We were full size once more. I'm sure Aunt Melissa's rollicking laughter was heard throughout the palace as Abracadabra sprang into the air.

The flight to the Himalayas was a beautiful one. And I was so proud to be standing next to Aunt Melissa when she presented the blue sapphire to the Grand High Lama.

On the way home from Tibet, we stopped to see the Parthenon in Greece and learned to dance the flamenco in Spain. And in London, we had tea with the Queen. Then we sped back across the Atlantic Ocean.

"I've had a wonderful time," I told Aunt Melissa, "but I'm afraid my parents are worried about me."

"They don't even know you've been gone," she replied. "From the time you left home, you have been traveling on *unicorn time,* where a day is no more than quick blink of the eyes."

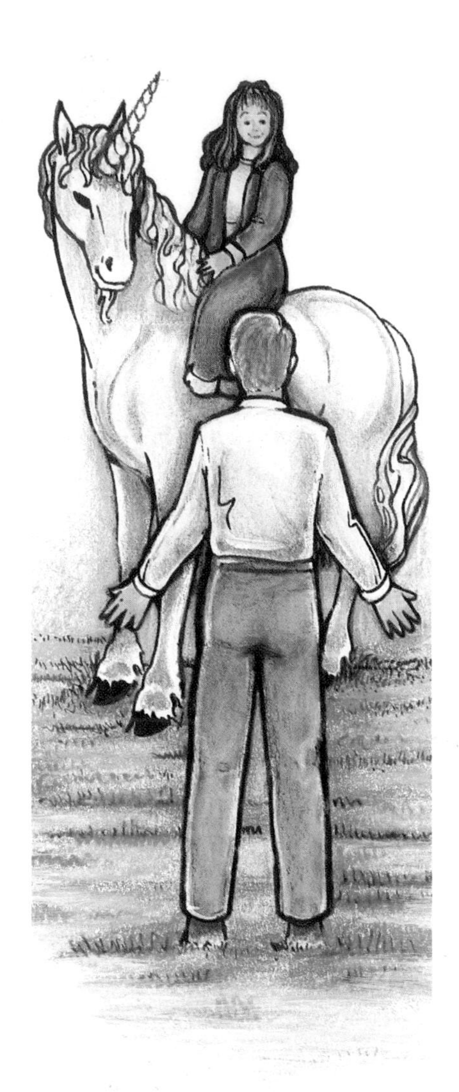

We arrived home early the next morning. When we reached our back yard, Abracadabra circled high in the sky, then slackened his speed and came in for a landing.

"What an exciting trip!" exclaimed Aunt Melissa, and she laughed gleefully as she slid from Abracadabra's back.

My father must have heard her, for he rushed onto the porch.

"What's going on here?" he wanted to know.

"Oh, nothing at all, George," Aunt Melissa giggled.

"Melissa!" he exclaimed. "When did you get here?"

"Don't worry," she replied. "I don't plan to stay long."

"Now, George, you know you're glad to see Melissa," my mother said as she stepped outside.

"Oh, of... of course," he stammered. "You're always welcome, Melissa. But what is that white moose doing in our yard again!" he grumbled, and he stomped across the grass for a closer look.

"This is my unicorn," I told him. "His name is Abracadabra. Come on, Dad, get on the unicorn with me, and we'll go for a short ride — just the two of us."

"Ride on a unicorn?" he asked in disbelief. "With that horn and all, it doesn't look safe."

"It will be the smoothest ride you've ever taken," I promised, and I took hold of Abracadabra's mane and jumped onto his back. "Come on, Dad!" I urged.

"Well... maybe just to the end of the block and back," he said, climbing up behind me.

At first Abracadabra moved in a slow, easy trot. Then he surged into a fast gallop and headed for the trees.

"Hold on tight, Dad!" I shouted. "Here we go!"

BOOKS FOR STUDENTS

– WINNERS OF THE NATIONAL WRITTEN &

A Chandrasekhar
age 9

Anika Thomas
age 13

Cara Reichel
age 15

Jonathan Kahn
age 9

Adam Moore
age 9

Leslie A MacKeen
age 9

Elizabeth Haidle
age 13

Amy Hagstrom
age 9

Isaac Whitlatch
age 11

Dav Pilkey
age 19

by Aruna Chandrasekhar, age 9
Houston, Texas

A touching and timely story! When the lives of many otters are threatened by a huge oil spill, a group of concerned people come to their rescue. Wonderful illustrations.

Printed Full Color
ISBN 0-933849-33-8

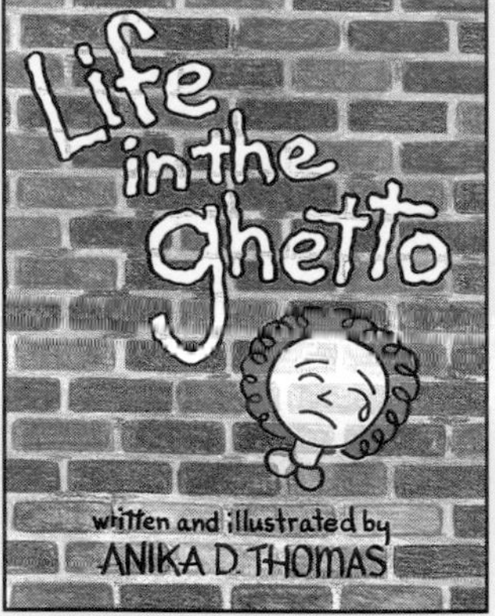

by Anika D. Thomas, age 13
Pittsburgh, Pennsylvania

A compelling autobiography! A young girl's heartrending account of growing up in a tough, inner-city neighborhood. The illustrations match the mood of this gripping story.

Printed Two Colors
ISBN 0-933849-34-6

by Cara Reichel, age 15
Rome, Georgia

Elegant and eloquent! A young stonecutter vows to create a great statue for his impoverished village. But his fame almost stops him from fulfilling that promise.

Printed Two Colors
ISBN 0-933849-35-4

by Jonathan Kahn, age 9
Richmond Heights, Ohio

A fascinating nature story! W Patulous, a prairie rattlesn searches for food, he must t avoid the claws and fangs of his enemies.

Printed Full Color
ISBN 0-933849-36-2

by Adam Moore, age 9
Broken Arrow, Oklahoma

A remarkable true story! When Adam was eight years old, he fell and ran an arrow into his head. With rare insight and humor, he tells of his ordeal and his amazing recovery.

Printed Two Colors
ISBN 0-933849-24-9

by Michael Aushenker, age 19
Ithaca, New York

Chomp! Chomp! When Arthur forgets to feed his goat, the animal eats everything in sight. A very funny story — good to the last bite. The illustrations are terrific.

Printed Full Color
ISBN 0-933849-28-1

by Leslie Ann MacKeen, age 9
Winston-Salem, North Carolina

Loaded with fun and puns! When Jeremiah T. Fitz's car stops running, several animals offer suggestions for fixing it. The results are hilarious. The illustrations are charming.

Printed Full Color
ISBN 0-933849-19-2

by Elizabeth Haidle, age 13
Beaverton, Oregon

A very touching story! The gr iest Elfkin learns to cherish friendship of others after he an injured snail and befrien orphaned boy. Absolutely beau

Printed Full Color
ISBN 0-933849-20-6

by Amy Hagstrom, age 9
Portola, California

An exciting western! When a boy and an old Indian try to save a herd of wild ponies, they discover a lost canyon and see the mystical vision of the Great White Stallion.

Printed Full Color
ISBN 0-933849-15-X

by Isaac Whitlatch, age 11
Casper, Wyoming

The true confessions of a devout vegetable hater! Isaac tells ways to avoid and dispose of the "slimy green things." His colorful illustrations provide a salad of laughter and mirth.

Printed Full Color
ISBN 0-933849-16-8

by Dav Pilkey, age 19
Cleveland, Ohio

A thought-provoking parable! Two kings halt an arms race and learn to live in peace. This outstanding book launched Dav's career. He now has seven more books published.

Printed Full Color
ISBN 0-933849-22-2

by Karen Kerber, age 12
St. Louis, Missouri

A delightfully playful book! Th is loaded with clever alliteration gentle humor. Karen's brightl ored illustrations are compos wiggly and waggly strokes of g

Printed Full Color
ISBN 0-933849-29-X

Your Students Will Love These Wonderful Book

BY STUDENTS!®

LLUSTRATED BY . . . AWARDS FOR STUDENTS –

yna Miller, age 19
nesville, Ohio

unniest Halloween ever! When ner the Rabbit takes all the , his friends get even. Their ous scheme includes a haunted e and mounds of chocolate.

d Full Color
0-933849-37-0

by Lauren Peters, age 7
Kansas City, Missouri

The Christmas that almost wasn't! When Santa Claus takes a vacation, Mrs. Claus and the elves go on strike. Toys aren't made. Cookies aren't baked. Super illustrations.

Printed Full Color
ISBN 0-933849-25-7

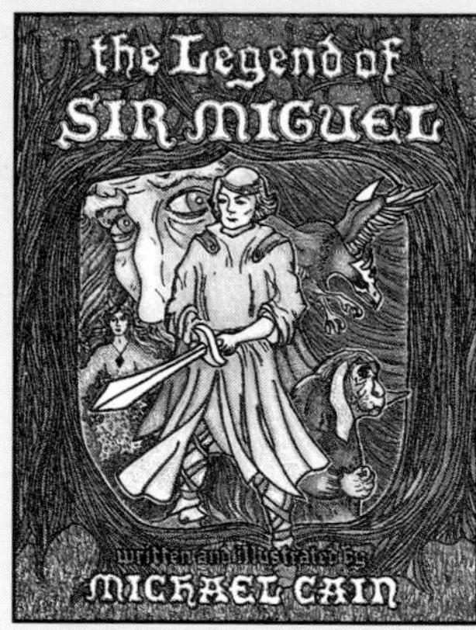

by Michael Cain, age 11
Annapolis, Maryland

A glorious tale of adventure! To become a knight, a young man must face a beast in the forest, a spell-binding witch, and a giant bird that guards a magic oval crystal.

Printed Full Color
ISBN 0-933849-26-5

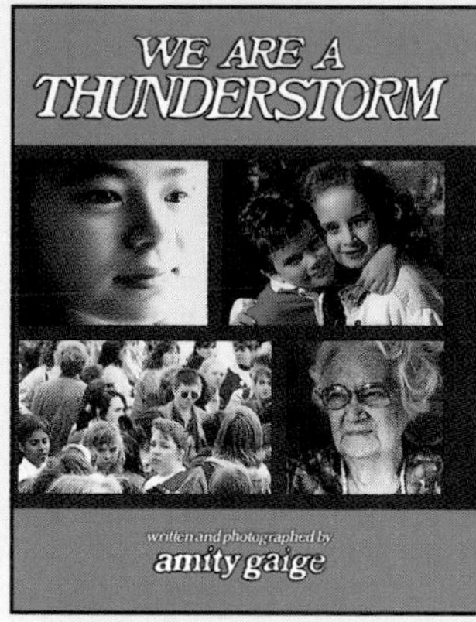

by Amity Gaige, age 16
Reading, Pennsylvania

A lyrical blend of poetry and photographs! Amity's sensitive poems offer thought-provoking ideas and amusing insights. This lovely book is one to be savored and enjoyed.

Printed Full Color
ISBN 0-933849-27-3

eidi Salter, age 19
keley, California

ky and wonderful! To save her imagination, a young girl must ont the Great Grey Grimly elf. The narrative is filled with nse. Vibrant illustrations.

d Full Color
-933849-21-4

by Dennis Vollmer, age 6
Grove, Oklahoma

A baby whale's curiosity gets him into a lot of trouble. GUINNESS BOOK OF RECORDS lists Dennis as the youngest author/illustrator of a published book.

Printed Full Color
ISBN 0-933849-12-5

by Lisa Gross, age 12
Santa Fe, New Mexico

A touching story of self-esteem! A puppy is laughed at because of his unusual appearance. His search for acceptance is told with sensitivity and humor. Wonderful illustrations.

Printed Full Color
ISBN 0-933849-13-3

by Stacy Chbosky, age 14
Pittsburgh, Pennsylvania

A powerful plea for freedom! This emotion-packed story of a young slave touches an essential part of the human spirit. Made into a film by Disney Educational Productions.

Printed Full Color
ISBN 0-933849-14-1

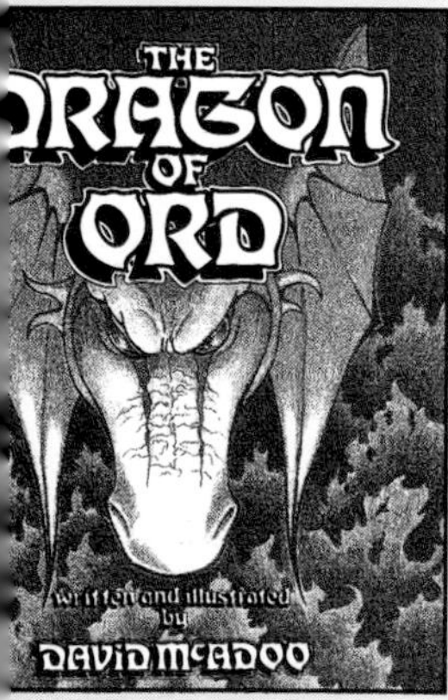

vid McAdoo, age 14
ingfield, Missouri

citing intergalactic adventure! distant future, a courageous r defends a kingdom from a n from outer space. Astound- pia illustrations.

Duotone
-933849-23-0

by Bonnie-Alise Leggat, age 8
Culpeper, Virginia

Amy J. Kendrick wants to play football, but her mother wants her to become a ballerina. Their clash of wills creates hilarious situations. Clever, delightful illustrations.

Printed Full Color
ISBN 0-933849-39-7

by Lisa Kirsten Butenhoff, age 13
Woodbury, Minnesota

The people of a Russian village face the winter without warm clothes or enough food. Then their lives are improved by a young girl's gifts. A tender story with lovely illustrations.

Printed Full Color
ISBN 0-933849-40-0

by Jennifer Brady, age 17
Columbia, Missouri

When poachers capture a pride of lions, a native boy tries to free the animals. A skillfully told story. Glowing illustrations illuminate this African adventure.

Printed Full Color
ISBN 0-933849-41-9

Jayna Miller age 19
Lauren Peters age 7
Michael Cain age 11
Heidi Salter age 19
Amity Gaige age 16
Dennis Vollmer age 6
Lisa Gross age 12
Stacy Chbosky age 14
Karen Kerber age 12
David McAdoo age 14

ey Will Want to Read and Enjoy All of Them! **ORDER NOW!**

THE WINNERS OF THE 1992 NATIONAL WRITTEN & ILLUSTRATED BY... AWARDS FOR STUDENTS

FIRST PLACE
6–9 Age Category
Benjamin Kendall
age 7
State College, Pennsylvania

ALIEN INVASIONS

When Ben puts on a new super-hero costume, he starts seeing Aliens who are from outer space. His attempts to stop the pesky invaders provide loads of laughs. The colorful illustrations add to the fun!

29 Pages, Full Color
ISBN 0-933849-42-7

FIRST PLACE
10–13 Age Category
Steven Shepard
age 13
Great Falls, Virginia

FOGBOUND

A gripping thriller!
When a boy rows his boat to an island to retrieve a stolen knife, he must face threatening fog, treacherous currents, and a sinister lobsterman. Outstanding illustrations!

29 Pages, Two-Color
ISBN 0-933849-43-5

FIRST PLACE
14–19 Age Category
Travis Williams
age 16
Sardis, B.C., Canada

CHANGES

A chilling mystery!
When a teen-age boy discovers his classmates are missing, he becomes entrapped in a web of conflicting stories, false alibis, and frightening changes. Dramatic ink drawings!

29 Pages, Two-Color
ISBN 0-933849-44-3

GOLD AWARD
Publisher's Selection
Dubravka Kolanovic'
age 18
Savannah, Georgia

A SPECIAL DAY

Ivan enjoys a wonderful day in the country with his grandparents, a dog, a cat, and a delightful bear that is *always* hungry. Cleverly written, brilliantly illustrated! Little kids will love this book!

29 Pages, Full Color
ISBN 0-933849-45-1

GOLD AWARD
Publisher's Selection
Amy Jones
age 17
Shirley, Arkansas

ABRACADABRA

A whirlwind adventure!
An enchanted unicorn helps a young girl rescue her eccentric aunt from the evil Sultan of Zabar. A charming story, with lovely illustrations that add a magical glow!

29 Pages, Full Color
ISBN 0-933849-46-X

BOOKS FOR STUDENTS BY STUDENTS!®

Written & Illustrated by . . .

by David Melton

This highly acclaimed teacher's manual offers classroom-proven, step-by-step instructions in all aspects of teaching students how to write, illustrate, assemble, and bind original books. Loaded with information and positive approaches that really work. Contains lesson plans, more than 200 illustrations, and suggested adaptations for use at all grade levels — K through college.

The results are dazzling!
Children's Book Review Service, Inc.

WRITTEN & ILLUSTRATED BY . . . provides a current of enthusiasm, positive thinking and faith in the creative spirit of children. David Melton has the heart of a teacher.
THE READING TEACHER

. . . an exceptional book! Just browsing through it stimulates excitement for writing.
Joyce E. Juntune, Executive Director
The National Association for Creativity

A "how to" book that really works.
Judy O'Brien, Teacher

Softcover, 96 Pages
ISBN 0-933849-00-1

LANDMARK EDITIONS, INC.
P.O. BOX 4469 • KANSAS CITY, MISSOURI 64127 • (816) 241-4919